MARRYING

MOUNTAIN MAN

HALLIE BENNETT

PROLOGUE

SHANNON

"Congratulations, you're going to be a beautiful bride."

"It must be great being engaged and owning a bridal shop. You get the first pick of new gowns!"

The cacophony of good wishes and congratulations weighs on my shoulders as my bridal shower wraps up. This should be one of the happiest days of my life, soon to be replaced by the actual happiest—my wedding day—but I can't shake the feeling of discomfort that's settled over me these past few months.

Like a gray cloud heavy with rain, it sinks deeper and deeper until sometimes it feels like I'm wading through a sea of fog. Aren't brides supposed to be bright-eyed and bushy-tailed?

No, those are squirrels.

But they should at least be excited to marry their fiancés. As the owner of Blushing Brides Boutique, I've heard my fair share of love stories, yet mine doesn't feel the way those women described.

Geez, what's wrong with me?

Whatever it is, I need to fix it quickly because I will be Mrs. Tim Grantham in less than a week.

Unless I shouldn't be?

I wander outside of the country club's reception room, signaling to my mom that I'll be right back as she works with the staff to clear the room of decorations and gifts. Drizzles of rain blanket the golf course, and my mood darkens accordingly with further contemplation of my lackluster relationship.

Tim proposed six months ago while we enjoyed dinner here at the club's restaurant. I ordered chicken marsala and ate all of the bread rolls. A blister was forming on the back of my ankle from my uncomfortable heels.

Memories of that evening burst at random in my mind like tiny champagne bubbles, but what I can't remember is a feeling of happiness. There was relief that he'd finally proposed after so many years. But did relief equal joy?

It almost felt like I'd finally completed the longest marathon of my life after dropping hints about rings and potential wedding venues. Our moms followed suit, constantly asking the direct question of when we'd get married and start popping out grandbabies.

Tim always shrugged with a secretive smile, and I humored his reluctance. Chalked it up to his determination to build his career rather than a marriage, since I'd been doing the same thing with opening Blushing Brides Boutique.

Starting a business in a small town isn't easy, but Suitor's Crossing's legend of love factored into my decision to start here rather than in a larger city. *Heart sparks* or soulmates abound in Suitor's Crossing. We have a romantic bridge from over a century ago where the myth originated—cross the bridge and you'll soon meet the person meant to be yours.

Or if you're already in a relationship, you'll know if they're your *heart spark* or not.

I can't say I've been brave enough to cross it with Tim.

We work so well together. Both driven and ambitious. Our parents are great friends and practically arranged our marriage long before Tim's family moved to Suitor's Crossing and we first met.

We make sense.

Even if our relationship lacks the sparks or magic that my friends have found recently.

Willow and Rhys.

Hannah and King.

Luna and Austin.

The list goes on and on.

"Ugh! Stop doubting your decision. It's done. You're getting married next week at noon," I berate myself, causing my dachshund, Melon, to lift his head from its resting position at my feet and stare questioningly at me.

"That's right. I'm becoming Mrs. Tim Grantham, and you're our ring bearer, and everything will be perfect."

So, why does it feel like I'm about to walk off a ship's plank and drown at sea?

CHAPTER ONE

D awn arrives red and ominous.

What's that sailor saying? *Red sky at night, sailors' delight. Red sky at morning, sailors take warning.* I've never been a sailor or particularly savvy with boats, but perhaps I should heed the sky's bad omen.

Because today's my wedding day.

After five years as a couple and six years before that as family friends, Tim Grantham and I are finally tying the knot.

Maybe.

Yes, we are.

Bracing myself on the granite counters of my kitchen island, I breathe deeply of my hot coffee and survey the explosion of frills and flowers littering my dining table before spilling over into the living room. Everything's set for an intimate ceremony in my backyard.

My parents wanted to host the wedding at the country club, but I refused. I love my cute cottage and adore the oasis I created outside—an oasis I'll be leaving behind once I move in with Tim. That had been one of our more heated arguments because he never considered leaving his townhouse for my home, insisting we'd need the extra space for future children.

Frustration threatens to rise again at the memory.

It's settled now, no need to upset yourself again.

Taking a fortifying sip of caffeine, my gaze lands on the cream wedding gown hanging by the window. Strapless despite my ample bust, the lace connects in the front in a row of pretty buttons that end right above my knee before opening into a slit.

It's sexy and form-fitting. Something people might disagree a plus-size woman like me should wear, but *fuck them*.

This is the dress of my dreams, and I'm gonna wear the hell out of it.

You're more excited about the dress than the groom.

Shut up.

My mom's veil rests on the dresser in my bedroom while a set of amethyst earrings lay waiting for me to don later—something old and something new.

Just need something blue.

Lucille should be awake by now, probably filling out another Sudoku puzzle with her cat, Percy, snuggled by her side. Seventy and sharp as a whip, she lives across the street in the cutest little bungalow with wisteria climbing its walls. She was the first person to welcome me to the neighborhood when I bought my home two years ago, and since then, we've shared Sunday brunch together, bonding over our love of puzzles. Sudoku for her, crosswords for me.

Shrugging off my robe, I toss it on a kitchen chair before turning around and heading to the front door. A garden full of flowers graces Lucille's backyard, including hydrangeas—my something blue—which she specially grew for my wedding bouquet.

"Care for a walk, Melon?" I rattle his leash as my feet slip into flip-flops.

Normally, I wouldn't go outside in mismatched shoes, dumpy pajamas, and bedhead, but who cares if I look like a hot mess? It's early, and it's only Lucille. She won't care either way what I wear.

Melon's tail wags frantically as he waits for me to attach his leash, and soon we're walking across the street. My knocking booms through the neighborhood, breaking the calm serenity of the cool April morning.

Tim's mom wanted me to be a June bride, but owning a bridal shop means my busy season is in full swing by that time. It honestly never crossed my mind to plan a June wedding on top of helping other brides prepare for their big day.

Too much stress.

Melon barks at my side. "Are you excited to see Miss Lucille? Ready for one of those treats she bakes—"

The oak door swings open but instead of a little old lady with purple hair, a giant man in jeans and a white tee shirt eyes me up and down like I'm the last bridal gown left at a warehouse sale. The flare of heat emanating from him causes all sorts of fireworks to ignite in my body.

"You're not Lucille." *No shit, Sherlock.* But my brain is fried with an overload of sensations. I stare dumbly at the flexing muscles of his exposed arms, the toolbelt around his thick waist.

Who the hell is this guy?

The poster child for *Handy Mountain Men R Us*?

"She's my grandma. She won't be back until Wednesday. Something about an out-of-town friend needing help." His piercing blue eyes travel over me again, and more warmth rises to the forefront.

Not the good, lusty kind either.

But the embarrassed because "I look like a crazy cat lady" kind.

I should've gotten dressed.

How were you supposed to know a hot handyman was in your future?

Why does it matter? You're engaged, remember?

Right, Tim—my fiancé.

"Maybe I can help you, though?" the stranger asks, casually leaning against the doorframe. Melon sniffs his boots before earning a scratch behind the ears from the man.

"Oh, um... Lucille said I could use her blue hydrangeas for my... She said I could use them," I finish lamely. The word "wedding" refuses to cross my lips. Like I don't want this man to know I'm destined to be someone else's wife before the day is done.

Are these normal bridal jitters?

Have I gone insane?

CHAPTER TWO

COLE

When Gran asked if I could take care of a few repair jobs around her house while she was out of town, I immediately agreed. My schedule was open, and I prefer fixing Gran's home myself rather than having her call another handyman in town. Not that I don't trust them, but this is my Gran. If anyone's going to fix her leaky faucet or loose shutters, it's going to be me.

What I didn't expect was a run-in with a curvy woman who looks like she just rolled out of bed. Who makes me want to tumble her right back into it—hair escaping her messy bun, bright rainbow-covered pajama pants, and all.

"Sure, come on in. I could use a break from wrangling her sink pipes into submission." She hesitantly steps inside, her wiener dog following to continue sniffing around my ankles. "I'm Cole, by the way. Cole Hammond."

"Shannon, and this is Melon."

Antique furniture and knick-knacks create a maze through Gran's home. As a boy, my mom always warned me about being careful, though that didn't prevent me from knocking over the random praying angel or picture frame. We trek through the living room to a set of French doors before emerging onto the patio with a pergola for shade.

Gran's green thumb is legendary in our family, considering how the gene ended with her, and her backyard showcases her talent to its best advantage. Flower beds, pruned bushes, and a vegetable patch create a natural sanctuary for all sorts of birds and other small creatures.

Pulling a pocket knife from my toolbelt, I gesture toward the hydrangea bush bursting in sapphire. "Do you have a preference for which buds?" I'm not a flower expert—they all look the same to me—but Shannon probably sees the different shades on the blooms, calculating which will work best for her needs.

"Any of them will do."

Okay, then.

A chuckle of surprise rises from my chest as I lean down and pluck a bundle of flowers with a sweep of my blade. "Is this enough?" The sensation of being a young boy delivering flowers on his first date runs through my mind when our hands touch in the exchange.

"Yeah, this should be good," she stutters out, her hand jerking back, letting the flowers tumble to the ground.

"Oh, sorry, I let go too soon."

"No, it's my fault."

We both quickly kneel at the same time causing our foreheads to bump together.

"Fuck!" Shannon's on the ground with a hand to her head as I crawl over to her. "Are you okay? Sorry about my hard head."

"It's fine. We both kind of... We're both at fault." She leans to the side and reaches under her ass, pulling out the crushed blooms beneath her. "These didn't survive, though."

"Guess it's a good thing Gran's got a ton of these flourishing bushes then. I can just cut you another bundle." And try not to give a concussion this time.

I help Shannon to her feet, holding her hands for a second too long, reveling in their soft feel against the rough texture of my palms. High-pitched yips vie for our attention as Melon carries the ruined hydrangea bundle away in his tiny mouth.

Unbidden, my thumb sweeps across Shannon's abused forehead. "Are you sure you're alright? That was a hard hit." I itch to test the softness of the wayward strands of hair cascading down the side of her head but resist the call.

"I promise I'm fine. It definitely woke me up, though."

"Yeah, it's kind of early to come over for flowers. Is it for anything special?" The blade of my pocket knife slices through another stem of flowers before I offer them to her for a second time. We're both prepared for the zap of energy that zings between us, though, as she accepts them without qualms.

"Oh, um..." She laughs a little, squeezing the hem of her oversized tee in her hand. "They're actually for a wedding."

My brows arch high at the admission. "Wow, who's the lucky couple?"

"Funny story..." Shannon avoids my eyes and a sick knot forms in my gut.

Fuck no. Don't say it.

"It's me." Her teeth dig into her bottom lip before she releases it with a sigh. "I'm getting married at noon today in a backyard ceremony."

"Today. Here," I repeat. It's like a pile of two-by-fours have fallen on my head. Everything becomes hazy while a dull pounding starts at the back of my skull.

"Yep. Well, not *here*, here. Across the street at my house. The one with the yellow door," she explains awkwardly, her hand vaguely gesturing toward the street.

I shouldn't be shocked she's engaged to someone else—a beautiful woman like her. The only surprise is that a man hasn't already tied her to him with his ring on her finger.

It's the pain in my heart throwing me for a loop. I don't know Shannon. She's a stranger. Yet, it feels like I've tumbled off a ladder and into a vat of paint—the thick, sticky substance clogging my nose and throat until I can't breathe.

Is Shannon my *heart spark*? Could she have been if I had met her first?

Wondering "What if?" kills me, and the question will hang in my mind for the foreseeable future.

"I should get going. Lots to do today." Shannon backs away, uncertainty clouding her features.

"Right." My head ducks down as I lead her through the house to the front door. I wish I could keep her here. Lock her inside and persuade her with my hands, my mouth, to stay. But she's got a man, and it's not me. The sooner it sinks in the better because pining after a girl I've known for fifteen minutes can't be my future.

Shit.

Unfortunately, as Shannon crosses the street, Melon in tow, I fear that's exactly what lies ahead of me.

CHAPTER THREE

Shannon

"What the hell was that?" I ask no one in particular once we return home. The blue hydrangeas weigh heavy in my hand as I hold my other palm up for inspection.

It's like Cole's still here, the imprint of his skin on mine failing to disappear. "That can't be good." Or at least, it's not good for Tim.

Because I think I just met my *heart spark*. Willow would squeal in excitement if she knew. For months she's been nagging me about the problems between me and Tim. How we don't act like soulmates. How we're only getting married to appease our parents.

Her objections to our engagement grew louder and louder until I had to ask her to stop before I said something I'd regret. Now it seems she may have been right. The lingering spark from Cole's touch is more powerful than anything I've ever felt with Tim.

Before my nerves get the best of me, I grab my phone and call my soon-to-be *ex*-fiancé.

It's crazy but meeting Cole was the push I needed to take the leap and finally call this farce of an engagement off. I've been afraid of disappointing my parents, worried I won't find anyone better than Tim. And honestly, a piece of my heart never truly believed in Suitor's Crossing's myth about soulmates.

Sure, my friends found love, but that could have been a coincidence, right? No need to credit a mysterious legend for the act. My practical mind wouldn't let me fully believe in *heart sparks*. But I also had never experienced anything to refute my beliefs until now.

"Hello?" Tim answers on the fourth ring. "Shannon, is everything alright?"

For a second, I close my eyes and hold my breath, waiting for a rush of confirmation either way. Does Tim's voice make me giddy? Does it erase Cole's presence? Or do I feel a sense of finality?

A bittersweet smile forms as I exhale. "Not really... Tim, I think it's a mistake for us to get married." There, it's out in the open now.

"What?" Disbelief and a speck of frustration tinge his voice. "I don't have time for your cold feet right now. We're getting married in a couple of hours. It's a done deal. Why don't you take a shower? Do whatever shit you've got to do to calm down, and when I see you later this afternoon, everything will work out. Okay?"

I hate his dismissiveness of my feelings. It's not new. He's done it before, but it really irritates me now, especially when I'm trying to have a serious conversation.

Probably should have done this in person.

Should have asked him to come over.

But after five years of being together, only for our relationship to crumble each progressive year—for my hope marriage would somehow save us and reignite the excitement to diminish—I just want this to be done.

"This isn't cold feet. Tim—"

"Baby, who is that? Come back to bed." A feminine whine echoes in the background, and I pull the phone away in shock before bringing it back to my ear.

"Who the fuck is that?" I ask. Not hurt that it appears he's cheating on me but angry as hell that he wants me to marry him hours after he's fucked whoever's in his bed right now.

"No one, Shannon."

"He didn't say that last night when my mouth was—" The disgruntled words are muffled as the call ends.

"What a fucking asshole."

Amazed at this turn of events, I wander into the living room and sweep all the decorations for later off the couch before flopping down to stare up at the ceiling. For a moment, I felt bad for breaking up over the phone on our wedding day, but now I wonder what would have happened if I hadn't gone over to Lucille's for those flowers.

If I hadn't met Cole.

I may not have called Tim. May not have seen him until this afternoon when we said our vows in front of our friends and family. None the wiser that he'd been sleeping with another woman this morning.

"We dodged a bullet, Melon." I pat the top of his head as he barks in agreement. Melon never really warmed up to him, even though I got Melon as a puppy and Tim's constantly been in his life. Melon just kind of tolerated him.

My dog had a better sense of the man I was going to marry than I did.

Your friends, too.

How am I gonna break this to our parents? Tim's mom and dad are actually nice—college buddies of my parents. Sucks that they have a douche for a son.

"I should call Sierra." The mention of my best friend grabs Melon's attention, his little nose lifting to the sky as if to sniff out her location. Sierra answers on the first ring a few seconds later.

"Your cake is fine," she says exasperatedly. "It's beautiful and will arrive at your house when I drive over in another hour or so."

Draping an arm over my head, I study the popcorn ceiling desperate for a renovation and sigh. "Well, the cake's welcome, although the wedding's off."

"What?" A scream of relief pierces my ear, and I hold my phone a foot away, rolling my eyes at her theatrics. "Fucking finally," she mutters when she finally calms down enough to speak. "You were cutting it close, breaking it off on your actual wedding day. What made you decide he wasn't good enough for you?"

Immediately, an image of Cole in his worn t-shirt and jeans forms. That crooked grin he gave me after opening the door is seared into my memory.

I don't know what to say.

Mentioning Cole seems kind of ridiculous. He's not the only reason things were called off, just the last straw to break the camel's back, so to speak.

Might as well tell her now. She'll hear it eventually.

The story spills out in spurts starting with meeting Cole this morning, my visceral reaction, and then the spark when our hands touched. The mention of sparks sets Sierra off on more loud squeals of delight, but when I get to the part about Tim cheating on me, a whole string of swearing follows.

"I can't believe the asshole's been cheating on you! Though it might explain why he took so long to propose..."

"Do you think I overreacted?" This is so far out of character for me. To be spontaneous. To make a decision without agonizing over every possible outcome. "Yes, there was a woman with him, and it sounded intimate, but maybe he was innocent?"

"Shannon, are you serious right now?"

"I've known him for a long time. He's been my boyfriend or fiancé for five years. Our parents are good friends. Maybe I should have given him the benefit of the doubt." It's not that I regret ending things with Tim, but I'm not usually this impulsive. I weigh the pros and cons of decisions for months on end sometimes. This kind of spur-of-the-moment action is new—freeing in a way I've never experienced before—but scary and unfamiliar, too.

Frustration growls over the phone line. I can just see Sierra in her bakery, hands on her hips, eyes heavenward as if praying for divine intervention to help me see the light. "Let's say, for argument's sake, he wasn't cheating. He was completely innocent. Or we'll imagine there wasn't even a woman there when you called. Would that change your mind? Would you still be marrying him today?"

"No." My prompt response brooks no hesitancy.

"Great. Then it really doesn't matter if he was cheating or not. I mean, it sucks, but you were already gonna break up with him. If you ask me, it kind of feels like you checked out of this relationship months ago and were just hanging on for your parents' benefit. Like, are you even hurt by his betrayal?"

I search my heart and mind for any pain and shrug, although she can't see it. "I'm... disappointed, I guess? I care about him, but I'm not in love with him. I suppose I haven't been in love with him for a while."

"So, we've established you're not in love with Tim. You haven't been for a while, and you're a newly single woman. Does that mean you're going to go back over to see that sexy handyman you felt sparks with?" The hopefulness in her voice is undeniable.

"Shouldn't there be a waiting period after you break up with your fiancé?" Although honestly, I kind of *do* want to head across the street and see Cole again. The image of my wedding dress hanging in the kitchen and all the wedding decor decorating my house right now makes me wish I was getting married still but with a different man entirely.

Instead of Tim in his traditional suit, Cole replaces him in his casual wear and a shiver of anticipation travels down my spine. Oh my god, I'm imagining marrying a stranger after a fifteen-minute interaction rather than my boyfriend of five years.

But couples do this all the time, right? Las Vegas is a thriving city of impromptu marriages. Besides, knowing someone for a long period of time doesn't necessarily guarantee a happily ever after. Lots of people, especially in Suitor's Crossing, marry after a week, a month, sometimes even a day, all because of *heart sparks*. They know when they've met their soulmate.

But you can't do that, I berate myself. *Can I?*

Could I really marry a stranger? My dress wouldn't have to go to waste today. Neither would Sierra's cake that she spent hours baking for me.

"We're already gonna have the pastor here, your friends, and your family." The logical taunts continue and unerringly my gaze trails out the window toward Lucille's cottage. Her grandson is somewhere inside tinkering around with those tools around his waist, and my thighs clench picturing what those jeans are hiding.

Oh my god, I'm gonna do this.

Afraid of losing my nerve, I blurt a rushed goodbye to Sierra whose knowing laughter vibrates through the line before I hang up and hurry to my bedroom to strip out of my pajamas and into something nicer—a sundress that hugs my curves and ends a few inches above my knee. Pulling out my hair tie, since it's barely holding much hair anymore, I shake out my tangled waves and run my fingers through it to make it a semblance of wild and free that looks sexy rather than electrocuted.

A quick swipe of mascara on my lashes and a swipe of lip gloss complete my look. The simple "girl next door going to propose to a man she barely knows" ensemble. Cosmetic lines are missing an entire demographic for their marketing. Nervous giggles erupt, and there's a sense of the Mad Hatter from *Alice in Wonderland* bouncing about in my home.

"Wish me luck, Melon." I smooth my hands down my sides after one last look in the bathroom mirror and smile. *Oh, crap. I need to brush my teeth.*

The doorbell rings a minute later after I gargle with mouthwash. Shit, did my parents decide to arrive early? Has Tim come over to try and woo me back? Or maybe it's Sierra coming to ensure I visit Cole before changing my mind.

Whoever it is, they're putting a serious crimp in my plans. Growling in annoyance, I huff towards the door and swing it open without peeking through the peephole first.

"Oh." All words freeze on my tongue. It's not my friends or family or my cheating ex. It's Cole standing before me with another bundle of flowers in his hands.

Is this fate?

A sign encouraging my current reckless path?

CHAPTER FOUR

COLE

I don't know why I'm here.

Shannon's an engaged woman, a stranger.

I'm not the type of guy who steals another man's woman. I respect boundaries and abhor cheating, yet my dumb ass is on Shannon's doorstep about to... what? Beg her to dump her fiance for me? Ask to attend her wedding in the hopes that my thick skull understands she's taken?

I don't understand what the fuck's going through my head. Something about this day has clearly scrambled my brain.

"Cole!" Shannon sounds breathless after the front door whips open. Melon runs out unheeded, scampering around my legs. "What are you doing here?"

She's changed since I last saw her. Gone are the pajamas and messy hair. Now, a sexy dress hugs her curves and reveals a shadow of cleavage.

Stop staring! She's not yours!

"I'm not really sure. Since you left, I haven't been able to get you out of my mind, despite knowing you're engaged. I swear I'm not this jerk who pursues taken women." I pinch the bridge of my nose in frustration. "Honestly, I should turn around and go back to my Gran's house, but there's something about you—"

Shannon launches herself at me, her arms wrapping around my neck and pulling me down for a hard kiss. My hands rise to grip her hips before freezing midair.

This is wrong.

No matter how right it feels, we can't do this.

Gently, I guide her back, breaking our connection. "Shannon, this isn't right. We can't—"

"I broke up with him."

"You what?" Surely, I didn't hear her correctly.

"I called Tim and broke up with him. Not just because of you, though." Her gaze drifts to the side before coming back to meet mine determinedly. "There were a lot of factors, but meeting you was the one that helped me take the leap."

Words refuse to form as a part of me is raising a fist to the air in victory while another is flattened by confusion. Oddly enough, I'm not freaked out by her declaration. If any other woman told me she'd broken off her engagement on her wedding day after just meeting me, I probably would have run for the hills thinking how unhealthy and clingy she'd be.

But something about Shannon is different.

Instinctively, I know this is out of character for her.

"So, you didn't love him?"

"Our parents have been friends forever. They wanted us together, and at first, it worked because we have similar ambitions when it comes to our careers. But no, I'm not in love with him. I've never loved him in the Suitor's Crossing way. Never *heart sparks*."

Relief is a cool river of water trickling down my back. Hearing how she isn't in love with her ex—how their relationship seemed more like an arranged partnership orchestrated by their parents makes this whole situation feel better.

"What's next for you?" I didn't come over here with a plan, so it's only natural I let her lead, considering the bomb she just dropped on me.

"My house is decorated. My dress is ready, and a pastor's on the way. I thought *we* could get married instead."

Did I say her breaking up with her fiancé was a bomb? Shannon basically proposing to me is a fucking meteorite crashing into the earth. Everything I thought I knew about myself is blown to smithereens.

Because I want to say "yes".

"You want to marry me?"

Her full lips open then close before responding, and she shuffles backward into the doorway. Her hands land on either side of the doorframe, the light pink of her tapping fingernails shining under the morning sun.

"In my head, it seemed romantic. Like a good idea. When you say it out loud, it sounds a little crazy. Maybe I was wrong—"

"No." I step forward, unwilling to let her retract the question. "I'll marry you, Shannon. I'll make you mine."

Hell yeah!

"Really?" Elation and hope transform her face as a mischievous smile spreads across her mouth.

"Really," I confirm.

She dips her head back and looks to the left inside her house before looking back at me. "The ceremony isn't until noon. We've got a little over two hours. My friends and family will probably arrive in that time, but what do you say we consummate this engagement? Best to make sure we're compatible, right?"

Damn, I like the way this woman thinks.

Marching forward until she retreats into the foyer, I call for Melon who runs inside before closing and locking the door. "I couldn't agree more." My t-shirt is quickly flung to the floor before I kick off my boots. Barefoot and bare-chested, I hold my arms out, palms up. "Come here, baby. Let's see how hot these sparks can burn."

Shannon throws herself into my arms, her legs wrapping around my waist as my palms cup her ass under her dress. She feels perfect in my hands. Like it's where she's meant to be.

Walking a few steps to the right, my hips pin her to the wall, and I grind my hardened cock into the warmth between her thighs. "Is this what you want from me, dirty girl? You need a man to satisfy this hot pussy?"

I thrust forward again, and the picture frames surrounding us tremble from the impact.

"Yes..." she moans.

Thank fuck. We don't have much time, and I want her just as desperate for me as I am for her. Drinking in the sight of her flushed skin, the bounce of her large breasts mesmerizes me. "Is this dress important to you?"

"What?"

"Is it your favorite? Does it have sentimental value?"

Shannon's brow wrinkles as her clouded eyes meet mine. "No, not really."

"Good." My hands rip the thin cotton in half from her neckline to her navel revealing curvy pale flesh unencumbered by a bra. Delicate veins lead to her tan nipples while little raised bumps surround the budded tips. Stretch marks hug her belly in pale lavender vines that I want to trace with my tongue.

"You're fucking beautiful. Do you know that?"

A self-conscious blush paints her chest in reds and pinks as she shrugs. "Sometimes, but it never hurts to hear."

I lean forward and allow my lips to graze her ear. A shudder quakes through her body at the contact. "Guess you'd better get used to it then because I plan on telling you every single damn day."

"Mmm..." Shannon hums in approval, her head drifting back to give me better access to kiss the rapid pulse beating at her neck.

In the past, girlfriends have described me as "too nice" or "boring", so relationships never lasted long. My momma and Gran raised me right—both strong women who taught me to respect and appreciate the ladies in my life—but those values rarely translated into a serious connection.

Girls in high school and then community college wanted a "bad boy", someone dangerous and full of adventure. Danger's a foreign concept in my world, but if given the chance, I could've provided adventure without needing to treat a woman poorly to keep her attention.

I'm not bitter about it. Hell, some good friends of mine would be considered "bad boys" by the women in town because they ride Harleys and are part of the Reaper's Wolves MC.

But it's a relief to hear Shannon's acceptance of compliments, to not get an immediate rebuttal accusing me of lying or a cynical eye roll.

A chime rings in a separate room. *One. Two. Three.* All the way up to ten. And I'm reminded of our limited time. There's no doubt we're compatible sexually, the chemistry singes everywhere our bodies touch, but I want to get my future wife off at least once before we're interrupted.

Want to prove she's not making a mistake choosing me as her husband.

First, by satisfying her physical desires, then learning how to sate her emotional needs.

CHAPTER FIVE

SHANNON

Rough fingertips tease the edge of my panties before sliding beneath the damp lace to find my clit. Cole circles the sensitive bundle of nerves, taps it, then continues down to thrust two thick fingers into my pussy.

"Goddamn, you're wet. Does the threat of someone walking in on us turn you on, dirty girl?" His short beard scratches as his head dips to suckle one of my nipples, an obscene slurping sound causing my pussy to clench around his fingers.

This is so wrong—fucking a stranger against the wall. Letting him call me his "dirty girl".

I'm a respectable woman, a successful business owner, and a responsible person all around. Yet Cole makes me feel naughty in the best way. Free and confident to conquer the world... or at least, *him*.

Sex has never been this all-consuming passionate affair. It's been perfunctory. Good to a point. These days, it's even scheduled because Tim and I didn't put much thought into its importance.

That won't be a problem with Cole, I can already tell.

"I'm not the only one affected by the threat of witnesses." My hand skims the heavy muscles of his chest and abdomen to cup the large bulge in his jeans. I massage it eagerly, desperate to feel its weight between my legs again, to have its girth stretch me wide.

"Seems you bring out a wilder side of me," he admits, and a supremely feminine pleasure fills my chest. What woman doesn't want to break the civilized control of her lover? Doesn't want to experience her man's savage dominance?

Unzipping his jeans, I urge the material lower and pull his cock free. "Care to demonstrate exactly how wild?" This seductress embodying my soul is new or perhaps she's always lived inside of me, waiting for the right man to draw her out, to coax her into playing.

Clearly, my ex was *not* that guy.

Cole replaces his fingers with the head of his cock then stops. "I don't have protection, but I'm clean. Are you sure you want to continue? We can figure something—"

"I'm sure." My hand digs into his shoulder and pulls him closer. Our labored breaths mingle in the sliver of space left between us. "Now, fuck me like a mountain man *should* fuck his bride. Hard and deep."

Suitor's Crossing is a small mountain town filled with bearded men in flannels and jeans—the quintessential mountain man—and Cole is no different. He may not have the plaid, but he's got the size and attitude. The hot-as-hell skill of working with his hands, the knowledge of how to use them effectively, whether it's repairing a dysfunctional drawer or caressing my touch-starved body.

A possessive growl resonates in the air when Cole plunges forward, burying every inch of his massive dick in my pussy. "My girl's got a dirty mouth, too? Damn, I'm a lucky bastard." He rolls his hips to grind his pelvis against my clit. "I'm gonna enjoy filling this cunt up every night and every morning, baby. I'll live for you milking me dry every time I shove this monster cock into this tight little pussy."

I have a dirty mouth?

Cole's words are trying to perform a miracle and make me come just from imagining our future together. Tangled up in bed. Bent over the couch. Even here for a repeat performance.

Long strokes form a harsh rhythm that slam my back into the wall, sending a picture frame careening to the floor, glass shattering in a burst of noise. It's distracting enough for me to break my focus on Cole and glance to the side, where I catch a glimpse of my parents parking on the curb.

No, not yet!

"My parents are here!" Panic seeps into my voice, but Cole remains calm. His only concession to the news is a grunt of demand.

"Come on, Shannon…" He encourages, increasing the speed of his thrusts as his hand returns to play with my clit. "Come for me now, unless you want them to meet your new fiancé with your pussy wrapped around my cock. Is it not enough that you'll be dripping with my cum, dirty girl?"

"Oh, god…" A depraved part of me doesn't care who sees us together. It's like Cole's erased my inhibitions, and I have no rational clue as to how. I just know that I never want to lose the feeling.

Sunlight glints through the windows bracketing my front door. My dad helps my mom unload the trunk of their car, arms full of wedding gifts before they turn to walk up my stone walkway.

A sharp slap to my clit refocuses my attention and another sets off an explosive orgasm. Tension clenches then releases. Sparks of bright pleasure burn the vestiges of my past away, leaving only a future imbued with possibilities.

I moan in satisfaction as Cole plants kiss after kiss on my lips, my cheeks, my neck—whispered compliments murmured against my skin. He gently lowers me back to the ground, and an errant appreciation for his strength flutters to life. I'm thick with curves, yet he held me aloft with no trouble. The realization has my body rallying for a second round, though my weak knees aren't on board.

I feel like a bowl of jello with wobbly legs and shaky arms. All I want to do is take a nap, but that's impossible with my parents ringing the doorbell.

"Just a minute!" Thank god, the windows are tinted to prevent people from being able to see inside the house. Despite Cole's filthy words earlier, I definitely do not want to introduce him to my parents while we're both half-naked.

"How do you want to play this?" Cole asks as he steps back, stuffs his glistening erection back in his jeans, and searches for his discarded shirt.

Shit, he didn't even come yet!

You'll make it up to him later.

My dress is beyond repair after being split down the middle. Not that I regret its ruin. Having Cole tear the material away from my body had to be one of the hottest things I've ever experienced, but it's damn inconvenient.

"Why don't you get dressed and hang out in the kitchen while I break the news?" I point down the hall where Melon's lapping at his bowl of water. Snagging a jacket from the coat closet, I zip the fuzzy material over my torn dress and wait for Cole to disappear from sight. As soon as he's gone, I unlock the front door and greet my parents with a harried smile, studiously ignoring the slickness between my thighs.

"Hey, you're early!"

Mom bustles inside with Dad following closely behind. "Your wedding is in less than two hours. I wanted to get here earlier, but the button on your father's dress pants broke. We had to... What are you wearing?"

Guess she finally noticed my odd attire.

"I'm cold," I say and fake a shiver. Casting a wary glance toward the kitchen where Cole's waiting, reality is an ice-cold bucket of water spilling over my head. My parents are going to have a conniption. My friends... Well, they might actually support my hasty decision to marry a stranger.

But everyone will voice concern over my headspace, I'm sure, because this is so out of character for practical Shannon.

"Mom, Dad, I need to tell you something."

"Everything alright?" The familiar baritone of my dad's voice comforts me, and breathing becomes a little easier.

"Yes and no." Wringing my hands together, I count to three before relaying the latest development in my relationship status. "Tim and I aren't getting married today. He was cheating on me. The good news is I still plan on having a wedding this afternoon. It'll just be to Lucille's grandson, Cole."

The hum of the heat kicking on buzzes in the background. Melon's rhythmic tip-taps down the hall grow louder as he nears. Each sound is amplified by the stunned silence of my parents.

"But you... and Tim..."

"Who's Lucille again?"

"She lives across the street. This is sudden, and I understand your confusion but what can I say? *Heart sparks* strike again." Hopefully, blaming the town legend will be enough explanation for now, since honestly, it's all I got.

"*Heart sparks*? That's what you're going with?" Mom scoffs, rolling her eyes heavenward. "What changed between last night's rehearsal dinner and this morning?"

She must have missed the part where I mentioned Tim's cheating in the shock of learning we're through. "For one, I learned he was cheating on me. But before that, I realized I don't love him like I should love a husband."

"But you love this... *Cole*? How long have you known him."

"Not long," I evade. "I feel more for him than I ever have for Tim. It's new, unfamiliar, but strong." Which is the truth.

"Ma'am, sir, if I may..." Cole appears in the entryway. He must've tired of hiding in the back, and I admire his courage to come out here. "Our relationship is sudden, but the timing doesn't negate how I feel about your daughter. Call it *heart sparks* or fate. All I know is I desire Shannon as my wife and promise to care for her the rest of my life."

It's a bold statement. One that sends my heart fluttering with giddiness like a crushing high schooler on her first date. Tim never declared himself so openly. Rarely expressed something so sentimental, and I didn't think it bothered me. But hearing Cole's words is like a balm to a wound I never quite realized I had.

Happy seems too tame a word to describe how I'm feeling, yet it's the closest approximation as I move to stand by my future husband's side—our two hands entwining into one secure bond.

CHAPTER SIX

COLE

"I need to call Tracy."

Shannon's mother stalks out the front door while her dad stares me down. It's not exactly a scowl, more of a curious examination, and it gives me hope that he's not immediately threatening to kick my ass for disrupting his family's life.

Once dressed, I knew I couldn't leave Shannon to deal with her parents alone. I'm no coward. A sense of rightness overcame me when I promised to be a true and kind husband. This is where I belong. Shannon's who I belong with, her hand in mine.

"Chris O'Reilly." Mr. O'Reilly offers his hand, and reluctantly, I let go of Shannon to shake it. "I won't pretend to understand what's going on here, but if my daughter's happy, then that's what matters most."

"I am, trust me. Happier than I've been in a while." Shannon hugs her dad as her mom reenters the room.

"Well, Tracy and Paul are stunned, to say the least. They're trying to get ahold of Tim to check on him." An aggrieved sigh follows her announcement. Her simple sheath dress is wrinkled around the waist where her hands crumple the material. "Make it make sense, Shan. Tim made a mistake with the cheating but don't throw away a relationship because of one mistake.

Relationships and *marriages*," she stresses, "are about compromise and forgiveness."

"Not when it comes to this. Not for me. Besides, it's about more than cheating. Tim wasn't my *heart spark*. He was the safe choice. To appease you and his parents. To make it easier for me to focus on Blushing Brides Boutique."

"We never forced you to—"

Shannon shakes her head. "It was never spoken aloud, but it's how I felt. I realize you're not used to me being so spontaneous but trust that I haven't completely lost my mind. Please believe that I know what I'm doing."

Mrs. O'Reilly gathers the gifts she left on a side table and addresses her husband. "Take me home, please. I need to lie down."

"You don't have to leave." Shannon tries to persuade her mom to stay but it's a fruitless endeavor. Her dad escorts Mrs. O'Reilly outside with an apologetic glance toward his daughter, the slamming of car doors filtering through the house.

"I'm sorry. We don't have to get married if you've changed your mind. I don't want to cause a rift between you and your parents." I almost choke on the words. Now that I've committed myself to Shannon, the thought of not marrying her today chafes. But family's important.

"She'll come around," Shannon says, sinking into the couch and helping Melon into her lap. "I expected resistance, though Dad took it better than I thought he would. I'm all in on us, Cole, no matter other people's opinions."

Kneeling before her, I pet Melon's skinny body as he rolls to his back. These two will be my new family. It'll be my responsibility to protect them. From physical threats as well as emotional ones like the judgment of others.

"So, what should we do next?"

Shannon smiles with gratitude and captures my hand with hers. "You should call any friends or family you want to attend while I notify the rest of the guests of the change. Oh, and a suit, if you have one." She lists a number of chores to complete in the short time before noon, the practical side of her coming out in full blast, and I admire this insight into what my future holds as her husband.

In quick succession, everything falls into place. My best friend Caleb shows up with coffee from his shop on Main Street while a couple of my friends from the Reaper's Wolves MC roar to a stop in front of the house. Unfortunately, my parents are on an anniversary cruise and my brother is away on business. Gran's too far away to drive back to Suitor's Crossing.

However, their absence won't stop me from making Shannon my wife. We'll just have another celebration when they return. Maybe when we make it legal by signing the marriage certificate we need to apply for—a small detail we'll iron out later.

"Didn't expect to attend a wedding this weekend," Caleb whispers from his place at my side as guests take their seats. Pastor Mullins clears his throat and opens his bible, studying passages he's probably recited thousands of times at weddings.

"Me neither, but the best things in life happen when you least expect them to."

The first strings of Mendelssohn's "Wedding March" float from a lone violinist's hands, and the French doors leading to the backyard open to reveal Shannon beautiful in a cream gown.

Tiny buttons form a line down her center, ending in an open slit at her thigh.

It's sexy and molds her curves perfectly, and I can't wait to rid her of it.

I've never given much thought to the kind of wedding I'd have. I assumed I'd marry eventually but it existed in the future, a hazy amalgamation of scenes from television or movies. This intimate ceremony eclipses those fictional imaginings.

Shannon's the prettiest girl I've ever seen in my life. Gorgeous in PJs and wild hair, breathtaking in silk and lace. A woman lightyears out of my league. Her shining indigo eyes meet mine and our gazes hold as she glides down the aisle, blue hydrangeas decorating the bouquet in her hands.

To think, those little flowers turned my world upside down.

When she reaches me, two words whisper in the air. "No regrets." It's a promise rather than a question.

"Never." My vow is equally hushed but no less serious.

"We welcome everyone to witness the joining of Shannon Elizabeth O'Reilly and Cole Alexander Hammond." Pastor Mullins recites a prayer and stresses the importance of not entering marriage lightly. A chuckle lodges in my throat as I maintain my composure. I'm sure he thinks we're flying in the face of his words considering how quickly we decided to marry.

"If any of you can show just cause why they may not be lawfully wed, speak now, or else forever hold your peace."

"I object!" Like a court scene on television, a man struts down the aisle, hand raised in the air. Fury outlines his rigid jaw and shoulders. A black tuxedo pinches and tugs on his body with every step, and it doesn't take a rocket scientist to figure out this is Shannon's disgruntled ex-groom.

"This asshole stole my bride!"

Immediately, I shift Shannon behind me as he marches forward to shout in my face. Gasps of dismay travel through the crowd like an ocean wave rippling toward the shore, and several guests nod in agreement, apparently siding with him.

"Tim, no one stole anybody. I broke up with you for multiple reasons, which you didn't care to listen to since you were too busy *cheating* on me with another woman." Shannon's voice should've turned the jerk to ice with its chilly finality, and ironically, my blood heats at her strength.

She's done taking his shit. Courageous enough to mount her defense in front of a dozen onlookers. Damn, I can't wait to get this over with so she can officially become my wife.

CHAPTER SEVEN

SHANNON

Tim is getting on my last nerve. What was he thinking showing up here like lyrics from a Taylor Swift song?

Maybe I should've expected his appearance but he hasn't tried calling me back after I hung up with him this morning. And he waited until the very last possible moment to arrive and wreak havoc on the ceremony.

Who does that? Not a man who claims to care for me, that's for sure.

"Shan, please... let's talk in private. We can work this out. Trust me."

I don't want to talk with him, but a twinge of guilt has me nodding in agreement. Even if we're over, he *was* my boyfriend turned fiancé for years, and despite his actions, I can still behave responsibly and have a mature conversation.

"Fine. You've got five minutes." I squeeze Cole's arm as I step around him, grateful for his protective stance the moment Tim began stomping down the aisle. "I'll be right back," I promise.

Titillated whispers and wide eyes follow me and Tim as we cross the yard and patio to enter the kitchen. Striding to the island, I make sure we're out of view of guests before crossing my arms and tapping my foot in annoyance.

"What are you doing here?"

"What am *I* doing here? I came to stop this farce." He runs a hand through his messy hair. "My mom called upset after hearing from your mom about the change to our wedding plans. I'm sorry you found out about Alicia that way, but it's over between us. Not that it was ever serious. Forgive me, so we can get married like we're supposed to. You've made your point with whoever that prick is outside."

God, what I wouldn't give to slap that superior smirk off his face.

The back of my jaw hurts where my teeth grind together, and my fingernails dig into my forearms to prevent me from doing something I'll regret, like hurling one of the oranges in my fruit bowl at his head.

"I'll call your mom to apologize. I didn't mean to hurt her, but we're not getting back together. We're not getting married. We have problems, Tim. Have had them for a while." I raise a hand to stop his rebuttal. "Don't pretend it's not true. You didn't decide to sleep with another woman because you're madly in love with me. We've been going through the motions, and I'm finally done."

"Shan..."

"Why do you even want to marry me? Why are you fighting this so hard?" That's the most confusing part for me. Tim's never been demonstrative in his feelings, yet he's chosen today to fight for our relationship.

Too little, too late.

"We're good together. We lead busy lives and don't see each other much but it works for us. We're equally ambitious when it comes to our careers. Our parents would love to see us together. Isn't that enough?" Confusion seeps into his voice.

"No, it's not." *Not anymore.* I may regret marrying Cole so quickly. Who can say what the future holds? But I would regret marrying Tim even more.

Because he doesn't make me feel the way Cole does.

Because this sense of rightness never settled when it came to Tim.

"You're serious. You're going to marry *him*. A fucking stranger. A nobody." He points outside to Cole's large frame patiently waiting for me to return to him. His casual suit jacket and slacks stretch over his broad shoulders, skim his thick thighs, and the urge to race back to his arms pulses in my blood.

"He's somebody to me—my future husband. Now, if you'll excuse me..." I sweep by Tim with my head held high and retrace my steps down the aisle. "Pastor, we're ready now."

The older gentleman glances between me, Cole, and the back of the house. I'm not sure if Tim's staying for the ceremony or not, but I couldn't care less. He's free to do as he pleases just as I am.

And I want to marry my handy mountain man.

Cole cups my cheek and studies my determined expression. "Are you alright?"

"I'm perfect. Tim shouldn't bother us anymore." *Fingers crossed.* "Let's get hitched."

After the early theatrics, the rest of the ceremony goes smoothly and twenty minutes later I'm Mrs. Shannon Hammond. Cole and I walk through a cloud of flower petals tossed over our heads as we head inside my house for a brief reception.

My missing parents weigh on my heart, but I know they'll come around once they see how happy I am. This wedding has been a burden on my shoulders for months. Get-togethers with my mom and Tim's mother were a constant barrage of ideas and gentle nudges toward a more extravagant ceremony. The likes of which neither woman had for their weddings.

Everything became this joint family effort rather than a celebration of two people in love.

It's amazing how clear things became once I met Cole.

"Two words: *heart sparks*." Willow steps to the front of the reception line with Rhys in tow. Both of them look blissfully in love in their coordinated outfits, which I'm sure are Willow's doing.

Rolling my eyes at her persistence, I accept her hug as Rhys shakes hands with Cole. "You were right. I was wrong. Happy now?"

"As long as you are. That's all that matters." She squeezes me extra tight before letting go with a knowing grin and letting the next guest congratulate us—Melon's veterinarian, Winston.

Yes, I invited my dog's vet, but it seems he knows Cole, too, by the way they're doing that whole one-sided man hug and pat on the back. Did everyone freaking know Cole aside from me?

Winston pulls a treat from his pocket and offers it to Melon, who's surprisingly acting very well-behaved despite the crowd of people. "I wish the three of you the best. Y'all are a cute little family."

"Thanks, man. I appreciate it." Cole slaps Winston's shoulder good-naturedly as a familiar face pushes into view.

"Congrats, girl!" Sierra hugs me close and whispers, "You are badass and incredibly brave. Although how can you be anything else when your new husband is hot as hell with that whole 'burly mountain man' thing he's got going on."

"Glad you approve." I laugh and hold her tight, thankful for her support. Sierra's been my best friend since kindergarten. Without my parents here, she's the next best thing since she's as close to a sister as I'll ever have.

"Take care of our girl," she warns Cole before turning away with a wave, scowling at the man behind my new husband. It's funny how I know Cole's best friend, Caleb, though I've never seen Cole before today.

Suitor's Crossing is a small town, but I guess it's not as tiny as it used to be.

Caleb owns Brewed, the coffee shop on Main Street, and he's Sierra's arch nemesis—her words—not mine. His cafe sits next to her bakery, Buttercream Dreams, and there's a constant battle waged between them for customers.

Caleb snags people with his delicious fresh roasts.

Sierra ensnares guests with her yummy pastries.

Both of them have mediocre substitutes for what their neighbor's known for—not that I'd tell Sierra I think her coffee sucks.

"What was that about?" Cole asks after noticing the glare Sierra shot Caleb's way. For his part, he just smirked at her obvious aggression and tipped his chin in acknowledgment.

"Don't tell me Caleb hasn't shared the Cold Coffee and Cakes War brewing between them?"

"That's Sierra Bear?" His head whips around to study Sierra more closely.

"Who's Sierra Bear? Her name's Sierra Kipley, the owner of Buttercream Dreams."

A bark of amusement tumbles out, and he scratches his cheek. "I'll be damned... That's the woman who's been giving

Caleb trouble, huh? She treats her shop like a mama bear does her cub, warding off potential threats—in this case, Caleb."

I roll my eyes. "You guys are ridiculous. She's just protecting her business interests, especially with the influx of chain restaurants lately." A popular coffee and donuts spot opened last month despite pushback from the town council, and already Sierra's feeling the slight decline in revenue.

"Whatever you say, *wife*." His tone changes from playful to desirous in the span of a second. The way he called me "wife" has my body tingling with need as I check the clock on my mantel.

One o'clock.

An hour-long ceremony plus reception? Not too shabby. And much preferred over a dragged-out affair considering everyone's gathered in my home.

"How bad would it be to kick everyone out, so our wedding night can start now?"

"Fuck..." Cole plants a hard kiss on my lips, eliciting a soft moan that I'm sure is heard by the loitering guests nearby. "Not bad at all. I'll make sure everyone leaves if you want to get ready."

Remembering how he tore my sundress earlier, I heed his advice and hurry down the hall with a mischievous grin. Part of me wants to keep my wedding dress on so Cole can tear it off, but I fucking love this dress and don't want to see it ruined.

My plan is to frame it and hang it in the hallway with the rest of the wedding pictures from our photographer. Kent Moreland sticks to local gigs these days, but he used to be a famous travel photog. His photos appeared in National Geographic and other notable magazines before he decided to retire to our little town.

I'm lucky he even agreed to shoot the wedding since I was afraid it'd be too far beneath him. But he was gracious and kind, content to document such a momentous day.

My wedding dress goes back to its hanger and into the closet as I study my reflection in the floor-length mirror leaning against the wall of my bedroom. Cream satin sculpts my abundant curves into an exaggerated hourglass, and I debate whether or not to switch to something else to preserve the lingerie when the door thuds open.

Too late to decide now.

My husky husband has arrived to claim his bride.

CHAPTER EIGHT

COLE

Ordering everyone out of Shannon's house was a breeze. Most people took one look at my stern face and towering height and decided to heed my command without delay.

My buddies clapped me on the back as they left, each of them sporting a knowing grin. It's no secret why Shannon and I want privacy. We want to fuck like the newlyweds we are.

Without an audience.

Without interruption.

Once I've locked the door behind the last guest and given Melon a pet on his sleepy head, I head toward Shannon's room like I've been here hundreds of times instead of just today. My heart stutters to a halt before shifting into high gear at the sight of Shannon dressed in only a corset and panties.

"Holy hell, how'd I get so lucky?" A guy like me—thick and "too nice"—never gets the girl in my experience. I make for a good friend, a handy man to have around when you need something fixed or hauled away, but women don't want me for forever.

Except for this woman who chose to marry me after our first meeting.

Heart sparks.

I knew they worked fast—provided instant connections—but to experience their magic is something else. I'll always be grateful to them and my Gran's impeccable timing. If she hadn't gone out of town this weekend, I may have met Shannon too late.

She says she would've broken things off with Tim anyway, but meeting me was the catalyst. If Shannon and I didn't meet until after today, who knows what state we'd be in?

She could be unhappily wed.

I'd be cursing myself for missing out on the woman meant to be mine.

"What are you thinking?" Shannon crosses the room and draws a line down my furrowed brow and nose to tap my lips. "You look less enthusiastic than I'd suppose a man should be prior to bedding his bride."

Circling her waist with my arms, I tug her into my chest and nuzzle her neck, enjoying the vanilla scent lathering her skin. "I was wondering what might have happened had you not gone to Gran's today. We wouldn't have met."

"Yet," she corrects. Her small hands map my chest, testing its firmness before unbuttoning my dress shirt. "Eventually, you would've visited Lucille while I was there, and the rest would be the same—the chemistry, the *heart sparks*. We may not have gotten married on the same day, but that's just due to convenient timing."

"You really don't think you would've married Tim today?" For some reason, my heart needs to hear confirmation again. She told me as much when I first knocked on her door. Proved her intentions when she chose me over Tim after his dramatic entrance during our vows.

But a piece of me still doubts the swiftness of her decision. Not that I think she's fickle or lying about her feelings, but my past isn't a great indicator of inciting such passion and interest from a woman.

Guess my wounded ego needs the boost.

"Hell, no. I like to believe common sense would've saved me from that mistake." My suit jacket and shirt fall to the floor as she works her way down to my belt and slacks, undoing the hooks and zippers to slide everything down to my ankles. The jut of my erection bumps her cheek, and Shannon eyes it curiously before glancing up at me.

"Cole, you can question what's happened or you can accept that I want you—*only you*—and let me suck your cock like the dirty girl you married. It's your choice."

Challenge thrown, she waits for my decision.

I'm not stupid. I know a good thing when I see it. When I literally have her kneeling at my feet promising heaven with her mouth.

Tangling my hands in the loose braid draped over her shoulder, I urge her forward with a grunt and nod. "Wrap those pretty lips around me, baby, and swallow deep. I'm thick and long, so your throat's gonna have to work me real good with that tongue of yours."

Lust sparks in her sapphire gaze as she licks her lips, leaving a shiny gloss before she follows my instructions. The stretch of her pink mouth surrounding my cock has me bracing a hand on the doorframe, crushing the wood beneath my palm in a harsh grip.

Shannon moans and bobs her head to a steady rhythm until the thick head of my dick hits the back of her throat.

"It's okay, baby. You can take it. Just relax and let these muscles do the work." Her head tilts back as I trace the undulating cords of her throat. "Dirty girls like you know how to suck cock. Understand how to please your man instinctively, don't you?"

She closes her eyes for a moment then opens them to reveal a wicked gleam. Slowly, Shannon allows me deeper, her fingernails digging into my thighs as she whimpers—the wave of vibration sending a lightning bolt of pleasure down my spine.

I allow her to find her own pace until it becomes too much and my balls draw up in preparation to unload in her hot mouth. "Time's up, baby. I want to finally come in your tight cunt, since we were interrupted earlier. There'll be time later for you to drink my cum, for me to paint your mouth and tits with my ownership."

The thought alone of Shannon covered in my cum almost breaks my restraint, but I reel it in, desperate for this first time as man and wife to go the way I want it to. Which means getting her off her knees and on the bed, legs spread wide for me to eat that pussy before fucking the hell out of it.

"But I wanted you to come in my mouth," she pouts, and it's fucking adorable. However, I've got other plans.

"Next time." I help Shannon to her feet and then guide her back toward the bed. "It's my turn to taste you."

"Really?" Excitement infuses her voice as she eagerly plops onto the bed and wiggles into the center spread eagle. Her enthusiasm's endearing as hell.

"Haven't you ever had your pussy eaten?" I'm not thrilled to hear about her sexual past, though it doesn't really matter when she now belongs to me, I suppose.

But Shannon's head shakes vigorously, sending her braid flying to the side. "No... Tim never saw the appeal and refused to even try. Honestly, that should've been a dealbreaker from the start. I don't know what I was thinking."

"You were trying to do what you thought right. Trying to appease your parents. Nothing wrong with that." I kick off my shoes and pants, so my movements are no longer hindered and crawl between her legs, using my shoulders to nudge her thighs wide. "Tim, on the other hand... Well, let's just say his mistake is my reward because I crave this sweet cunt. To lick and suck all this delicious cream."

My fingers drag through her saturated folds before plunging into her pulsing channel. Shannon arches her back with a cry and bunches the bedsheet beneath her hands.

"God, yes!"

Dark curls part to reveal the shining blush of Shannon's pussy, and my mouth practically waters as I breathe in her sweet arousal. Wrapping my arms under her legs, I tug her forward until my beard rubs against her inner thighs. "I'm gonna make this so good for you, baby. My dirty girl's gonna love my tongue fucking this tight cunt."

Bending lower, I lick up her center before landing on her clit. The little bud throbs beneath my tongue as I flick it over and over in tune with Shannon's breathy cries. Like a man lost in the forest, a hunter searching for his prey, I devour Shannon's soft flesh with nibbles of my teeth. My fingers circle her opening before thrusting deep to find that special spongy spot inside that makes Shannon shudder in response.

"That's it. There's my dirty girl. Ride my face. Fuck yourself on my tongue. The quicker you give me your orgasm the sooner you'll have my cock filling you up, stretching this little pussy until you can't walk tomorrow."

Shannon's nails scrape at my shoulders as she bucks into my mouth, grinding against my lips and searching for release. One of my hands pinches the ass cheek I'm holding, and I relish the moan of pain mixing with pleasure as Shannon finally lets go.

"Cole!" she shouts. "Oh my god!" I help her ride out the climax, licking and petting her until she collapses back on the bed. Sweat gleams on her skin as my mouth glides over her round stomach to her plump tits. I pepper tender kisses around her nipples before tweaking them between my fingers.

"You did so well, baby. Are you ready for your reward?" I notch the head of my cock against her opening and lift her leg to brace it against my shoulder, her knee resting against my ear.

"Oh, fuck," she gasps. "I'm surprised my body can even do that. But I suppose when you're boneless and your muscles are liquid, you can do anything."

"I promised to stretch you out good," I tease, although I search her expression for any note of pain. I don't want to put her in an uncomfortable position. I just want her as open as she can be to accept every inch of my massive cock.

"Go on, then. Show me who's boss, *husband*." She tries clamping her pussy around the inch I've given her, and I growl at the seductive tone in her voice.

"Seems you've recovered quite nicely. But I should have known my dirty girl can't stay down for long. You're too hungry for cock, aren't you?"

"Too hungry for *your* cock." The clear devotion in her tone has my soul singing her praises, and my heart pounding in my chest.

"As you wish." Bending forward with a grunt, I bury myself deep but don't stop there. Immediately, I rear back to thrust again. hammering into her until she slides up the bed and braces her hands against the headboard.

Her juicy tits jiggle with every movement, and once again, I'm drawn to their lure. Ducking my head to suckle their puffy tips, reveling in the color change from tan to dark mauve.

"God, you taste so good," I murmur.

"You *feel* so good."

And I won't ever let her forget it.

Shannon is mine now and forever, no matter what happens. She's my wife, and I'm her husband.

Fuck Tim.

Fuck her parents if they never come around.

Fuck anybody who thinks to tear us apart because of the way we got together.

I'll defend our relationship until the very last breath in my lungs because Shannon's my *heart spark*, my soulmate.

"Cole, don't stop... Don't..." Shannon's breathing becomes shallower as my hips circle and grind against her clit, my muscles laboring to pump her cunt full with my cock and seed. *One, two, three...* And an explosion of heat rips through my body as we come together. Groans and cries of satisfaction fill the room, and I even hear Melon howl outside the door, causing us to laugh as we collapse into one another.

"That was... Wow," Shannon says, turning to rub her hand over my chest, her nose burrowing into my neck.

"Yeah, it was."

"And to think, we get to do that as often as we want." A girlish giggle erupts from Shannon, and I adore her excitement. Adore *her*, period.

"Give me a second, and we'll go for round two."

"Promise, husband?"

"Promise, wife."

And I make good on my words for the rest of the night.

EPILOGUE ONE

SHANNON

ONE YEAR LATER

It's hard to believe I've been married for a year. Time's flown by since my impromptu decision to marry Cole, but it's proven to be the best decision of my life. I love my handy mountain man, and he loves me.

It's actually kind of annoying how blissfully happy we are.

"Any special plans for your anniversary?" Lucille asks us as she sips her lemon tea. Cole's Gran practically jumped out of her matching cardigan set when she heard the news of our marriage, she was so happy. Then, when she revealed her true purpose for leaving Suitor's Crossing that weekend—in the hopes that the two of us would meet because of my need for something blue—well... Let's just say she hasn't stopped touting her matchmaking skills for all and sundry to hear.

I asked her once why she didn't invite Cole over for one of our brunches if she wanted us to meet so badly, but she said it needed to be done a certain way. Whatever that meant. I'm just thrilled it worked out in the end.

"It wouldn't be right for me to share the surprise with you before my own bride, Gran." Cole plays with the loose strands of my hair and grins. He loves teasing his grandma, loves his entire family, actually.

Everyone accepted me into the fold without question, and eventually, my parents fell in line once they saw Cole and I were together for the long haul. Tim's parents haven't quite forgiven me yet, but it doesn't bother me like it used to.

They're my parents' friends, and they all still hang out. So as long as they're happy, I am, too.

"Oh, you sly boy..." Lucille shakes her head and caresses her cat, Percy, while Melon naps at her feet. "Can't an old woman live vicariously through her grandchildren? Tales of your exploits keep me young."

"Your own exploits keep you young," I retort, well aware of the shenanigans she and her friends get up to at the senior center. Sierra delivers batches of cookies every Friday evening and hears all the gossip.

A frail shoulder rises and falls beneath a lavender cardigan. "Perhaps... Now, would you two be dears and fetch me some more hydrangeas for my vase?" She gestures toward a wilting bouquet next to her. "It's time for a refresh."

"Yes, ma'am." Cole stands, stretching his arms high overhead until a sliver of skin is revealed below the hem of his tee shirt. Flushing with sudden heat, I follow him outside and sneak a hand under the cotton.

"Excuse me, miss, but I'm a married man." He winks and then spanks my ass as I wrap a finger in the loop of his jeans.

"Good thing I'm the wife, then." I go on my tiptoes to press a kiss to his waiting mouth, never able to get enough of him. Cole's a constant aphrodisiac for my libido, and time together doesn't seem to dampen its strength.

His large palms circle my neck and tip my chin back to take charge of the kiss before mumbling, "You realize Gran's watching through the window, right?"

"Yep, but I don't mind. Let her have her fun, she deserves it. After all, she gave me you."

"Mmm... You're right." He nips my bottom lip before licking the sting away. "She gave me the love of my life. I owe everything to her."

"So, let's give her a show."

Suddenly, Cole sweeps me backward over his arm in a grand gesture, and I laugh at his ridiculousness before he swallows my amusement with a kiss for the ages. A whoop sounds from the cottage along with a bark.

My life is different than it was a year ago. More fun. Filled with love.

And I wouldn't have it any other way.

EPILOGUE TWO

WINSTON

"Gremlin, no!"

The cafe quiets as my Siberian Husky races toward a curvy brunette and snatches the napkin-wrapped cookie from her table. A couple of customers laugh, but my wayward dog's victim isn't one of them. Instead, frown lines deepen around her mouth and eyes as she glares at me and Gremlin, who I've finally caught now that he's occupied with his sugary prize.

"Sorry about that. He's still learning his manners." *And always will be since he's a stubborn as hell husky.* But I keep that last part to myself.

"He shouldn't be off-leash in a restaurant. He shouldn't be in here at all," she huffs, picking up the ripped napkin on the floor, sans cookie, before gathering her purse and coffee tumbler. Her slicked-back no-nonsense bun shines under the fluorescent lighting, making my fingers itch to ruffle it with my rough hands, an inappropriate urge I barely resist.

What the hell?

"You're right. But he slipped his collar and ran straight for the smell of food. Let me buy you another cookie—or two—to make up for it." Maybe she'll let me sit with her, and we can chat. Maybe I'll figure out why my body's vibrating like a tuning fork all of a sudden, despite the obvious "leave me the fuck alone" aura emanating from her.

"That won't be necessary. I'm leaving and shouldn't have had another cookie anyway." She shrugs into a puffy jacket, and I take a moment to admire her lush curves before they're zipped away from view. *Damn, she's pretty.* Even if she does seem a bit uptight.

Gremlin, hungry for more treats, noses at her pockets until she skitters away and bumps into another table.

"Gremlin, sit." My firm tone registers, and he listens, but it's clear the damage is done. I should've been keeping a better hold on my dog instead of ogling the pretty girl before me.

"Again, I'm sorry. He's extra—"

"Winston! Come on, man, no dogs allowed," Caleb, the owner of the coffee shop, calls from behind the counter. Another apology's on the tip of my tongue when the woman veers around us and escapes the awkward moment. Through the shop windows, I watch her hop into a gray sedan before pulling out and driving down Main Street.

Fuck.

Gremlin and I return to the sidewalk outside Brewed, and a strange part of me regrets not getting her name or number. I usually don't go for women who don't seem comfortable with animals, since they're a huge part of my life as a veterinarian. Problem cases like my husky—a rescue before he came home with me a month ago—fill a lot of my time.

Women who can't handle that kind of life? They're not for me.

And this girl definitely fits the bill. She didn't greet Gremlin. Didn't even ask to pet him. So, despite my attraction to her soft curves, it's for the best that I didn't press for more from her.

At least, that's what my mind says.

My gut instinct on the other hand... Well, that's a different story.

DON'T MISS WINSTON'S STORY NEXT IN
PURSUED BY THE MOUNTAIN MAN!

THANKS FOR READING & DON'T FORGET TO RATE/ REVIEW!

Please consider leaving a rating/review. Ratings & reviews are the #1 way to support an indie author like me.
The more reviews, the more my books are shown to other potential readers!
And they serve as guides to readers on whether to take a chance on an indie author.
I appreciate your support!
XO, Hallie

BOOKS BY THIS AUTHOR

Every Hallie Bennett book features a curvy girl & a filthy-talking hero!
Find Hallie's entire catalog at www.thearrowedheart.com!

ABOUT THE AUTHOR

Hallie prefers steamy, insta-love stories where curvy girls are claimed by filthy-talking heroes. And when she ran out of reading material, she decided to write her own stories. If you want a quick, hot read, she's your girl!